CATHY HOPKINS

The Valentine's Day Kitten

With illustrations by
Joëlle Dreidemy

Barrington Stoke

For Georgia, my silver cat
who inspired the story

First published in 2017 in Great Britain by
Barrington Stoke Ltd
18 Walker Street, Edinburgh, EH3 7LP

www.barringtonstoke.co.uk

Text © 2017 Cathy Hopkins
Illustrations © 2017 Joëlle Dreidemy

A CIP catalogue record for this book is available
from the British Library upon request

ISBN: 978-1-78112-678-3

Printed in China by Leo

CONTENTS

CHAPTER 1
Operation Find Misty

Ellie got out her notebook and came to sit next to me on my bed. "So, Miss Muller," she said, "just how long have you been having the dreams?"

I laughed because she looked so serious. Ellie is my best friend and she wants to be a detective when she leaves school. She reads endless crime books and watches all the TV shows her parents will let her about missing people, murder and theft. We've been friends since we met at the school gates on our first day of Year 7, over a year ago.

We're in Year 8 now and, in that year, Ellie has wanted to be a vet, an airline pilot, a rock star, a creator of cupcakes and now ... a detective. I wondered how long this new ambition was going to last. If I knew Ellie, she'd probably change her mind next week.

"I've already told you about the dreams, Ellie," I said.

"This is for my official records and the chart," Ellie said.

She pointed at my bedroom wall where she'd pinned a photo of my kitten Misty. My missing kitten. Mum and Dad had got her for me last year just after Valentine's Day. I'd been feeling left out because all my mates – even Ellie – had got a Valentine's card. There wasn't anyone I liked, but I'd hoped that I'd

get one from some mystery admirer. But no.
Nothing.

Mum and Dad saw how disappointed I was
and the next day when I got home from school,
there was a white box with a turquoise bow
waiting for me on the kitchen table. Inside was
the most adorable kitten I'd ever seen. She
was only ten weeks old with silver grey fur. I
picked her up and she nuzzled into my neck. It
was love at first sight. Just the thought of that
moment made my eyes fill up with tears.

"The dreams that you've been having might
lead us to Misty," Ellie said, as persistent as a
real-life detective. "When did they start?"

"Um ... about a week ago," I said. "Last
Saturday."

"The night after Misty disappeared?"

"Correct, officer."

Ellie gave me a stern look. "You're not taking this seriously."

"I am," I said. "That's why I called you officer, officer."

"Call me Detective Inspector then," she said. "Exactly what happens in the dreams?"

"It's always the same," I told her. "That's what's so strange. But like so many dreams, it fades when I wake up."

"Tell me what you remember."

"OK, um ... there's a place – an old hotel. I know my way round, like I've been there before. There's a boy, a painting."

Ellie was busy scribbling. "Boy. Can you describe him?"

"Teenager. Dark hair. Kind of cute. Oh ... er ... it's really hard to remember, Ellie. He fades too when I wake up, but I'm pretty sure he likes painting."

"Evidence of this?" she asked.

"I think I saw him at an easel in one of the dreams and, and ... there's a painting by him in the hotel, but I'm not sure what of so I don't know how I know that and ... yes, I'm sure, in fact, that Misty is sometimes on a chair in the room he's in."

Ellie nodded. "Interesting. Very interesting," she said. "Is the room at the hotel or somewhere else?"

"Ooo. Don't know."

Ellie sighed and tapped her notebook. "Anything else?"

I shook my head. Just the thought of Misty made me want to cry. It was my fault she'd gone. She was a naughty kitten, always getting into places she shouldn't be and always losing her collar. The week before she disappeared, she'd lost it again and I hadn't replaced it.

"Yes," I said. "Misty had no collar on. I hadn't got round to going to the pet shop to buy her a new one. I kept meaning to and –"

Ellie saw that my eyes were wet with tears. "You mustn't blame yourself, Marcie," she said, and her voice was kinder now. "Don't worry. We'll find her."

She ripped the page out of her notebook, got up and stuck it to the wall. "There. I've made a plan," she said. "Misty has to be somewhere. What I propose is that we copy her photo and put it up everywhere. Someone must have seen her."

I wiped my eyes. "Mum already did that the day after Misty disappeared."

"Ah. Then I should interview her in case she has any important clues."

I shook my head. "I can tell you now that she hasn't," I said. "Nothing. Misty might have been stolen. She's such a pretty cat."

Misty had liked to sit out on the wall at the front of our house. People always stopped to admire her as they went past. She was friendly too, and so she purred and nuzzled people's hands when they gave her a stroke. Someone could have taken her, no bother.

"Then we'll find the thief," Ellie said. "Someone must have seen something. In the meantime, these dreams you've been having are trying to tell you something."

I wished I had Ellie's faith. I'd told Mum and Dad about my dreams and they said it was no wonder I dreamed about Misty every night – she was so dear to me. Mum told me not to let the dreams upset me.

"My grandma said that the best way to remember dreams," Ellie went on, "is to write them down first thing in the morning. Before you get out of bed, before you brush your teeth, before you do anything. That way, they don't fade away. You must try and remember the details – anything. We need an identikit of this boy for our wall chart. He might be real. He might be the thief and that's what your dream is trying to tell you."

"What?" I said. "Like the colour of his hair, his eyes –"

"Exactly. Height, age, everything you can remember. The hotel too. Try and remember what it's called and where it is. Can you do that, Marcie?"

I gave her a salute. "I can give it a try, Detective Inspector."

Ellie started to pace around the room. "Let's sum up the plan of action. Number one –

dreams. Marcie to make note of details. Two –
put new photos on lamp-posts in case rain or
other elements have spoiled them. And three,
contact the local vets and the local cat and dog
home. I've seen it on telly. Often these places
are where people go about missing animals,
lost or found."

I looked up at the wall. Ellie had written
'Operation Find Misty' in capital letters on a
sheet of paper and was now busy updating her
plan. She stopped and pulled her long blonde
hair into a fresh ponytail, then got back to
work.

*

Mum was great. As soon as Ellie had gone
home she got on the case and began ringing the
animal rescue centres.

"I'm calling to report a missing kitten," she
said into the phone. "One year old. Silver grey.
Very fluffy. Answers to the name of Misty."

She looked over at me and then said in a lower voice, "And before you ask, she wasn't wearing a collar."

I sat at the kitchen table next to her and listened in as Mum went down the list we'd made of local vets and rescue centres. With each call, I felt my hopes rise then fall as Mum shook her head and clicked the phone off.

"I'm sorry, love," she said when she'd finished her last call. "But they said cats often turn up weeks after they've gone missing, so not to give up hope."

But I felt hopeless and so disappointed. I got up to go upstairs and cursed myself for the 100th time for not getting Misty a new collar. If she ever did come home, I'd go to the pet shop and buy at least 20 new collars. In the meantime, all I could do was try and remember my dreams for Detective Inspector Ellie.

CHAPTER 2
Dream Diary

"Marcie, it's seven thirty, time to get up," Mum called from the other side of my bedroom door.

Before I got out of bed, I found the notepad under my pillow. Ellie had been right. If I wrote down my dreams before I did anything, before I was even fully awake, I did remember more. As the week had gone on, the images had become clearer and clearer.

The first morning that I'd woken after Ellie's visit, my dreams were hazy. The second

13

morning, I'd remembered more. By the third, I could see the boy's painting in the hotel. It was a painting of two people on a hill in the countryside and it had a distinctive style, modern, almost abstract, and in strong bold colours.

And now I had a name for the boy.

I opened the notepad and began to write.

'Boy's name – Ryan. Age – about 14, could be 15. Clothes – jeans, grey hoodie. Painting in the hotel is by a desk in a study or office. Misty is in a different room – maybe a bedroom.'

Ellie would be pleased with me. She was good at art and she had started her identikit drawing at school in the lunch break. She added details of Ryan's clothes and looks as I gave them to her and soon a picture of a real boy was appearing on the page.

I was so busy scribbling that I didn't notice Mum come in.

"Come on, sleepy head," she said. "Marcie, what *are* you doing?"

"Doing?" I shoved my notepad back under my pillow. "Nothing."

"Don't lie," Mum said. "You were writing something."

I sighed. If anyone should have been a detective, it was my mum. She never missed anything. I sat up, sighed and told her about writing down my dreams.

Mum reached out and took my hand. "Marcie love, I know Ellie means well, but a dream is a dream. This is the real world – here, now. I know you're worried about Misty and we're doing everything we can to find her, but putting your faith in dreams is just nonsense –"

"But, Mum," I said, "Ellie says –"

Mum shook her head. "I don't want you to pin your hopes on something that's going to lead nowhere, love. It was a good idea of Ellie's to contact the vets and rescue homes – that was something useful we could do – but dreams aren't real."

"But, Mum, I have to do something."

"It's still early days, love. We might hear some news from one of the vets."

I felt myself getting tearful. If no one had found Misty, she might be out in the cold somewhere, hungry and afraid. The thought of her like that freaked me out. In the dream, she was in a strange room, but at least she looked safe. That thought gave me some hope and comfort.

Mum sighed. "I'm worried about you," she said. "I know it's been hard for you since we lost Misty but ... don't get obsessed with these dreams, will you? Life has to go on." She stood up and went on, "And you, young lady, have school to go to. Now come on, get up and I promise I'll ring around the vets again to see if there's any news."

I did as I was told. Maybe Mum was right. I was kidding myself that dreams were going to lead me to my kitten. Misty was gone and I had to accept that. I decided I'd do my best to put the boy and the hotel and the painting out of my mind and focus on doing what I could in the real world – and I could go out and look for Misty every night after school.

But as I got dressed, I felt empty and sad. Misty had always been there in the morning, asleep on the end of my bed, getting under my feet as I got ready for school then waiting on the window sill or the front wall when I came home in the afternoon. Her absence had left a big hole in my heart and I didn't know what to do about it.

CHAPTER 3
Party Time

"I don't want to go," I said to Ellie as we stood in front of my wardrobe and rooted around to see what I could wear. It was Saturday morning and we were getting ready to go to my aunt's 40th birthday party on the other side of town. It had been in the calendar for months but, since Misty had disappeared, I'd forgotten all about it. "The last thing I'm in the mood for now is a party with a bunch of oldies," I moaned.

Ellie started doing mad hippy dancing. "At least I can come with you and I bet there'll be a disco."

"Oh my god, I hope my dad doesn't join in," I said. "He can be *so* embarrassing."

"You never know, the party might be fun and your dad's dancing will at least take your mind off Misty," Ellie said.

She went over to the window and looked out at the dark sky. The weather forecast had warned of snow. I hoped it was wrong. Misty would never survive out there if it froze. She'd always picked the sunniest spot in the house to lie in and often curled up under a radiator when the heating was on.

"It's two whole weeks now since Misty disappeared and we haven't got a single lead," I said. "It's as if she never existed."

Ellie sighed. "I know." Even she had run out of ideas.

"We're leaving in ten minutes," Dad called up the stairs.

I pulled on my only party dress and brushed my hair. Ellie came to stand next to me as we looked in the mirror. "We look like Rose Red and Rose White," she said.

We did. Ellie's hair was in a messy fishtail plait and she was wearing a white dress and silver Converse hi-tops. I had long hair too, but mine was dark and curly, and I was wearing my red dress and my red Converse.

Ellie gave me a hug, then took out the fancy lip gloss she'd got for Christmas and we both put a bit on. Then we sprayed on a blast of my perfume. I grinned at Ellie. She had lifted my gloomy mood and by the time we were ready to go, I felt much more in the party spirit.

We heard Dad honk the car horn outside.

"Party time," Ellie said, and she danced out into the hall and down the stairs.

*

The snow started as we drove into town. Big soft flakes floated down and made the streets and houses look like a white fairyland. When Dad turned off the main road and headed up a country lane, I began to wonder where he was going.

"Isn't the party at Aunty Jen's house?" I asked.

"Didn't you look at the invite, Marcie?" Mum asked. "No. This is a big birthday and she's having her party in a hotel. No expense spared."

In the back seat, Ellie raised an eyebrow. "Cool."

I stared out of the window at the winter wonderland. *Please, please don't let Misty be out in this*, I prayed.

Moments later, we turned off the lane, past big stone pillars and up to an old country hotel. It looked picture perfect in the snow and I felt my spirits lift a little more.

Dad dropped Mum, Ellie and me at the front door, then went off to park the car. We dashed inside and a smart woman came forward to take our coats. Mum was straight off to greet relatives and as I looked around at the wood-panelled walls and old-fashioned décor, it hit me.

"Ellie," I whispered. "This is the hotel."

"I know. It's lovely, isn't it?"

"No, I mean yes, it is lovely but it's *the* hotel."

"*The* hotel?" she said.

"Yes, the one from my dreams."

Ellie's cheeks grew pink with excitement. "Are you serious?"

I nodded. "I know this place. I recognise it."

"Have you been here before?" Ellie asked.

"I don't think so." I pointed across the wide hall. "That leads to the dining rooms on the right and there's a bar to the left which opens out onto a terrace."

Ellie was off to check. "You're right," she called back. "There *is* a bar and look, there are the dining rooms."

I followed her down the corridor. "It might not mean anything. It might be that I saw the place on a travel show on TV or something."

"Did your mum and dad have a leaflet for the hotel?" Ellie said. "Maybe you saw that but then you forgot."

"No," I said. "*No*. I would have remembered. I didn't even see the invite, that's why I didn't know where the party was going to be held."

"Right," Ellie said, back in her Detective Inspector mode. "This is excellent news. We need to make some enquiries." She marched back into the hall and up to the desk. I almost ran after her.

"Excuse me, but does a boy called Ryan live here?" Ellie asked, in her brisk, confident way.

The woman behind the desk shook her head. "No. No one of that name."

"Who owns the hotel?" Ellie went on.

"It's just been taken over by new owners, Mr and Mrs Webb."

25

"Do they have children?"

"No children. Just them."

"Do they have a cat? A kitten?"

The woman smiled. "My, you have a lot of questions," she said. "No. No cats or kittens, just an old border collie called Alfred. Can I ask why you want to know?"

"Oh, we're looking for a lost kitten and we think a boy called Ryan might be able to help," I said.

The woman looked puzzled now. "And why did you think they might be here?" she asked.

I saw Dad coming in and I pulled Ellie away. "Oh, no reason. My friend here has all sorts of mad ideas."

The woman rolled her eyes, then went forward to greet Dad.

Ellie and I ran to the Ladies, where we could talk in private.

"What do you think this means?" I asked.

Ellie was thinking. "Not sure yet. Tell me about the dreams again."

"There's this hotel. This one, and I know my way round it. It wasn't snowing in my dreams. Oh! The painting. I keep going back to the painting in the dream. A landscape."

"Would you recognise it?" Ellie asked.

"Yes."

"OK," she said. "Two things. First, Ryan might be a guest at the party so when everyone has sat down, we should have a good look at the boys."

"Hah. Any excuse," I said.

Ellie gave me her stern look. "This is business, Marcie. Second, the painting. Let's look for it. I spotted loads of paintings on the walls in the corridor and bar. You take the ground floor and I'll take the upper floors."

"But you won't know what to look for," I said.

"Good point," she said. "OK, we'll go together."

We went back out along the corridor where we found Mum looking frantic. "Where have you two been?" she asked. "Come on. Jen is wondering where you are and we're about to sit down for our meal."

Ellie and I swapped looks.

'Our search will have to wait,' I thought, as we followed Mum into the dining room.

*

Once we were seated, Ellie and I scanned the tables for boys. There was a lad with ginger hair on the table next to ours. Not Ryan. A boy with dark hair on the table in the corner. No, too young. A boy with a floppy blond fringe in the other corner. No.

"Is he here, Marcie?" Ellie whispered.

"Don't think so," I replied.

Dad had overheard. He winked. "Checking out the talent, hey, Marcie?"

I went bright red. "I was not. I was just seeing who's here."

Dad grinned. "OK. If that's your story."

I felt so embarrassed and decided to concentrate on the plate of food in front of me. Some sort of cheese thing in pastry. I took a bite. It should have been tasty, but it felt like I was chewing old cardboard.

"What is the matter with you two?" Mum asked after they had served the pudding. It was chocolate mousse with raspberry sauce, but I was so desperate to start looking for the painting that I had no appetite. "Marcie, you've hardly touched a thing. And, Ellie, you look like you've got ants in your pants."

Ellie giggled. Unlike me, she'd eaten every scrap and was eyeing my plate too. "Actually, we're dying to go exploring," she said. "I love old places like this and ... um, we're doing a project in school about buildings from the 18th century."

"But this one is 16th century or so," Mum said.

"Oh yeah ... 18th, 16th, old, that's what I meant," Ellie blustered. She didn't like getting caught out when she was being a detective.

But Mum had stopped listening, because the waiters were beginning to push the tables back to make a dance floor.

"Time we made our exit," I said, "before the dad dancing starts."

"May we, Mrs Muller?" Ellie asked. "We'll just have a look round before the light goes." Ellie looked at the big clock on the wall. It was five o'clock and starting to get dark outside.

"Very well." Mum sighed. "Off you go, but don't be long and make sure you're back when we cut the birthday cake."

We were off in a flash. I'd already checked out the paintings in the dining room while we were eating. There were just a few boring landscapes and one of a man in old-fashioned clothes who looked like he'd sucked a lemon. There were none that looked like Ryan's bold, modern style.

In the corridor was more of the same – paintings in ornate gilt frames, all dull and brown with age.

We were about to head up the stairs when the receptionist appeared. "Can I help you ladies?" she asked.

'Get out of this one, Ellie,' I thought.

"I, we, are looking for someone," Ellie said.

"I remember, a boy called Ryan and a cat. The upstairs is for guests of the hotel only," she said.

"Oh, but just about everyone at the party is staying here," I told her. "It's my aunt's 40th. I said I'd fetch a cardigan for her friend."

The receptionist looked as if she was just about to ask for more details when a guest appeared at the front desk muttering about the snow and the roads. She went off to greet him and Ellie and I dashed upstairs before she could stop us.

We searched the corridors. We searched all of the open rooms. Nothing.

"If there is a painting," Ellie said, "it could be anywhere."

"There *is* a painting," I said. "And the more I go round this hotel, the more I feel I know it."

Ellie looked at a room in front of us. The number 14 was on the door. She sighed. "The bedrooms are all locked. Your painting could be in any one of them and no way will they let us in them."

"I don't think it is," I said. "I don't remember it in a bedroom. I –"

"OK," Ellie said. "Stop. Think. Remember. Close your eyes. Breathe. Relax. Take your time. It will come to you."

I did as Ellie said. I took a deep breath. I could see the painting in my mind's eye. A wall. A room. It didn't look like a bedroom.

"I ... I don't think it's upstairs," I said. "I get the feeling it's downstairs. A study. Yes, that's it. Near the ..."

"Near the what?"

"Near the kitchen I think," I said. "I don't know why but that's what my instinct is telling me."

"Then let's go with that," Ellie said.

We headed downstairs again and smiled our brightest smiles at the receptionist, as if that would stop her suspicious looks.

"I'm not going to ask her which way the kitchen is," Ellie whispered, "in case she has us arrested."

We headed back to the dining room and watched which way the staff were going with empty plates.

"That way," Ellie said, and she pointed to the back of the hotel.

We followed a waitress down a corridor then into an area that said 'Staff Only'. We checked to see if anyone was watching, then began to look into the rooms. There was a cupboard full of cleaning materials, another full of sheets and blankets, and then we came to a room that looked like an office.

"Oh, wow!" I gasped.

"What?" Ellie asked.

I pointed to the wall behind a desk cluttered with files and papers. There was the painting from my dreams. A scene with two people on a green hill.

Ellie strode into the office and peered at the painting.

"What are you doing?" I hissed.

"Signature," she said. "I'm looking for a name."

I went to join her. "There." I pointed to the right-hand corner. "Something's written there."

Ellie had a closer look. "It's not a name, it's two capital letters. R.C."

"R.C. The boy's name was Ryan. R."

Ellie punched the air then pulled out her phone and took a photo of the painting. "Evidence," she said. "Now all we need to find out is where this painting came from and where he – this R.C. – is."

"Can I help you?" a stern voice behind us said.

We turned to see a man with a grey beard and glasses.

"I, er … we …" I blustered.

He looked friendly, but serious at the same time. "Might I ask what you're doing in my office?"

"Oh, we got lost," I said. "We're at my aunt's party and we were looking for the Ladies."

"All the way down here?" the man said. "It's right by the dining room."

"Oh. OK. We're so sorry," Ellie said. She started to turn on the charm. "I'm Ellie and this is Marcie. Marcie is Jen's niece."

"And I am Mr Webb, the owner of the hotel."

"Excellent. And what a lovely hotel it is," Ellie said. "I ... we ... couldn't help but notice the painting above your desk. You don't know who did it, do you?"

Mr Webb shook his head. "I don't. It came with the hotel when we bought it."

"What about the previous owners?" she pressed. "They might know."

"I doubt it," he said, and he gave Ellie a bemused look. "They moved to Australia when they sold us the hotel and left all the paintings."

In the distance, I could hear people singing 'Happy Birthday to You'.

I grabbed Ellie's arm. "They're cutting the cake! Mum will kill me if we're not there for that and the group photo." I pulled her away. "Come on. Sorry to have disturbed you, Mr Webb. Lovely painting."

Mr Webb laughed. "Thank you, Marcie. Now get back to your party."

*

"It's a *clue*," Ellie said, as we raced back along the corridor.

I shrugged. I was disappointed. "Maybe, but it doesn't tell us anything. And yes, I know we could try and contact the last owner, but if they're in Australia that could take weeks and it would be so complicated. We're still no closer to finding Misty."

"That's where you're wrong," Ellie said. "I have a plan. If R.C. did this painting, I bet he's painted others too. I took a photo – remember? So all we need to do is go round all the art galleries in town, show the photo and ask if anyone has heard of him. It's a small place and there can't be that many artists. We'll go after school on Monday."

She paused for breath, then went on. "This is how detective work unfolds. A clue at a time and you just have to follow them. You in?"

I nodded. "Of course I am, but I'll have to think up some excuse. I don't want to tell Mum and Dad about this. They think I'm crazy enough as it is."

CHAPTER 4
Looking for Ryan

"We've been in five different galleries and my feet are sore," I groaned.

It was Monday after school and Ellie and I had raced into town with our list of local galleries.

"Only three more to go," Ellie said, and she pointed over the road. "You do the one over there, I'll do the one on Broad Street and we can do the last one together."

I knew I had no choice with Ellie in charge and so I set off and opened the door into a bright, light gallery where rows of huge paintings of fruit were hanging on the white walls.

I went over to the super chic woman sitting at a clear glass desk in the corner. "Excuse me," I said. "I'm looking for an artist but I only have his initials – which are R.C."

"What sort of work does he do?" the woman asked.

"Um. Not sure. I've only seen one – a landscape."

"OK," she said. "I can't say R.C. rings a bell but I'll look in our list of artists."

As she searched her contacts, I had a look at the fruit paintings on the wall. I didn't like them very much.

"No one with those initials on my list," the woman said. "Have you tried Hepworth's?"

I nodded.

"And Bentalls?"

"Yep."

"I'd try and get the whole name," she said. "That might help."

I thanked her and went back out to the street where I could see Ellie waiting for me.

"Any luck?" she asked.

I shook my head. "Nope."

"Me neither and the last gallery is now a coffee shop."

"So what now?" I felt so dejected and close to tears.

Ellie put her arm round me. "Hey, come on," she said. "Don't cry."

"I'll try not to, but we're clutching at straws," I said as we set off for the bus stop. "And Misty is still missing."

As we waited for our bus, I spotted a new gift shop with lots of notices in the window. Ellie went over for a closer look, then pointed at a poster.

"Hey, look at this," she said. "It's a competition for Valentine's Day. You have to write a poem or paint a picture and they'll display them in the window. Then they'll put the winner's work on sale here." She peered in. "Look, they sell paintings and stuff. Let's go inside."

I didn't follow her. I'd had enough disappointment for one afternoon and felt even sadder now I'd been reminded of Valentine's Day. Misty had been my Valentine's Day kitten.

And, sure enough, Ellie came out five minutes later and shook her head. "Sorry. They haven't heard of R.C. either."

"I was remembering how I got Misty for Valentine's Day last year," I told her.

Ellie nodded. "I remember too."

"Best Valentine ever."

Ellie looked back at the window. "So, why don't you write a poem about her and enter the competition?"

I glanced at the shop. "What good would that do? Anyway, they probably want poems about people, not kittens."

Ellie shrugged. "Who says there are rules? You love Misty. She loves you."

CHAPTER 5
A Poem for Misty

When I got home, I couldn't stop thinking about Ellie's plan that I should enter the competition. I'd never been in love, never even met a boy I liked very much and who didn't annoy me – though I guessed that one day I would. I looked over at the photo of Misty on my bedroom wall. Ellie had been right as usual.

'You're my Valentine, Misty,' I thought.

I spent the rest of the evening writing, crossing out, writing again and by bedtime, I'd finished.

The Purrfect Companion

You're not a normal Valentine,
you're furry with a tail.
But you're the sweetest friend I ever had
and my love for you will never fail.

After school the next day, I went back to the gift shop. Before I went in, I read the entries in the window. There was the usual mush about how roses are red and violets are blue and there were a couple of drawings of flowers and hearts. Nothing about kittens. I almost walked away, but the young man with a beard behind the desk had seen me and waved me in.

He had a friendly face so I took a deep breath, went in and handed him my poem. "I know it's not very good," I said, "but it's about my kitten and I do love her as much as any Valentine."

He smiled as he read my entry, then he took down my contact details and put them on the back of the poem. "We've never had one about a cat before," he said, "but I understand. My dog, Jeffers, he's my best friend and he loves me to the moon and back."

"So did Misty. She was always there for me," I said and I told him about how Misty had gone missing.

He listened sympathetically. "I think it's lovely you've written a poem about her," he said when I'd finished. "I do hope you find her again."

"Me too," I said.

*

Two days later, after school, I got a call from Ellie. "Get down here right away," she said.

"Where? Why?"

"The gift shop. You have to see this."

"Just tell me –" I started, but Ellie had hung up.

I grabbed my coat and got down to town as fast as I could. Ellie was waiting for me outside the shop. She pointed at the window. "Look."

There was a new entry in the window display. A painting of a silver grey kitten. I recognised the style straight away and, there to confirm it, were the initials R.C. in the corner.

"Oh!" I said. "It's him."

Ellie's eyes were bright with excitement. "I know. Let's go in."

We opened the door and went over to the counter where a teenager, with pink streaks in her hair, was chewing gum and looking bored.

"The painting," I said. "In the window. The one of the kitten. Who did it?"

The girl looked over at us. "Dunno. Some lad came in with it about an hour ago."

"Who? What did he look like?" I asked.

"Dark hair. He was wearing a hoodie I think. I didn't take much notice."

"Can you find out?" I said. "Please," I added, in case I sounded a bit rude. "When I entered the competition, the man who was here put my address on the back of my poem."

"Nah," she said. "I don't work here normally. It's my uncle's shop. He never said to get an address."

"Will he be back?" Ellie asked.

"Not today." A boy came in behind us and the girl's face lit up as she waved at him. "Got to go. Locking up early."

"Please," I begged. "Can't you just look to see if he put his address?"

The girl sighed and went over to the window. "Nah. No address."

"Phone number? Name?"

"Nah. Nothing," the girl said. She was still chewing her gum. "You'll have to come back when my uncle's in tomorrow. He might know."

The boy opened the door. "Come on, Sal," he said.

Sal ushered us out. "Laters."

I wanted to punch her.

"We're getting closer," Ellie said when we got out on to the street. "Don't worry about him not leaving his details. He's bound to go back to see if he's won. He wouldn't have entered otherwise."

I stood and stared at the picture in the window. It was Misty, without a doubt. For the first time in weeks, I felt hopeful. If this mystery boy had her then she was safe. All I had to do was get her back. I grinned at Ellie. "Maybe my dreams *have* led us here."

Ellie nodded. "All we had to do was follow the clues." She looked in the window and grinned back at me. "And that, my dear Marcie, is one cute kitten and one big fat clue."

*

We went back the next day, and we were lucky. Sal's uncle was there. I told him how we thought the painting in the window was of Misty.

"Sal's a sweetheart, but I could kill her for not getting his address," he said. "I told her to take contact details for all the entrants but she's such an air-head she never listens. Don't you worry. I'll keep my eye out. The closing date is Valentine's Day, which is only two days away. He's bound to be in touch to see if he's won. I promise I'll ring if there's any news."

Wednesday went by.

Thursday.

Friday – Valentine's Day – and still no news. I was beginning to lose hope when my phone rang. It was the Sal from the shop. "That R.C. boy's been in," she said. "I've got his address and a phone number."

"Did you tell him about Misty?"

"What?" she said, and I could hear her chewing her gum down the phone. "Nah, it was my uncle who was here when he came in. Have you got a pen?"

I scribbled down the address she gave me then ran to the kitchen and told Mum. Instead of leaping for joy, she looked worried.

"I thought you'd forgotten all about those dreams, Marcie," she said. "But now look what's happened. You can't just turn up at someone's house out of the blue. I'm not even sure that girl in the shop should have given you the address. Besides, there are lots of silver grey cats in the world, not just Misty."

"Please, Mum, please," I begged. "I know it sounds mad but I have to do this."

She shook her head. "No, Marcie. You're not going to a stranger's house and I'm not going off on some wild goose chase."

I got down on my knees. "Mum, I'm begging you. It's not a wild goose chase. It's a kitten chase and what have we got to lose? I promise from the very bottom of my heart that I shan't get upset if it's not Misty but we *have* to follow this up. Please. Please. *Please*."

For some reason, the sight of me begging on my knees made her laugh. Parents are peculiar beings. She sighed then said, "OK, give me the number."

I got up from the floor and stood over her as she called the number that Sal had given us.

"No answer," Mum said after a few moments.

"Can we go there?" I begged again. "Please. We can leave a note if they're not in." I was about to get back down on my knees, but she stopped me.

"OK." Mum sighed again. "Let me get my coat."

"And can we pick Ellie up on the way?"

"OK. But I mean it, Marcie, be prepared for disappointment. This boy might have painted his own cat or he might have painted a cat from his imagination."

"I know. I know," I said, but deep inside I just knew it was Misty and it wouldn't be long before we would be together again.

CHAPTER 6
Mystery Boy

The journey seemed to take for ever. The address we had was for a village just out of town and Mum took a few wrong turns along the way. At last, we saw Willow Road and stopped in front of a white cottage. Number 5. We'd arrived.

As we got out of the car and walked to the front door, I realised I had no idea what to say or who I might meet. Either way, I was going to sound like a mad person with my talk of dreams and clues and poems and kittens.

Mum seemed to have realised this. "Let me do the talking," she said as she knocked on the front door.

No answer.

She knocked again.

Still no answer.

In the meantime, Ellie had sneaked away and was peering in the front window.

"Ellie! Get back here," Mum said. "How would it look if someone comes back and finds us sneaking about in their garden?"

Ellie looked sheepish but she did as she was told and came back to the door.

"We need to leave a note," Mum said, and she took a bit of paper and a pen out of her bag. "We'll leave our phone number."

"There might not be anybody in," Ellie said, "but Misty might be."

"If it is Misty that this boy drew," Mum said.

Mum wrote her note and put it in the letter box. "I suggest we head back home and see if anyone calls," she said, then went and got back in the car.

We'd got so close, I couldn't bear to leave. I bent down by the front door, opened the letter box and called, "Misty, MISTY, are you there?"

"Marcie, come away," Mum shouted, "right now!"

I called one last time – "*MISTY!*" – but still couldn't hear anything and so I called again.

"Marcie, I mean it. Now!"

I looked over at Mum. I could tell by her tone that she meant business, so I got up and walked back to the lane.

"Ellie, get in the back," Mum told her. "We've tried. We've left our number and now we're going home. Marcie, you too. Now!"

I got into the car and looked back at the house. Just as Mum started the engine, I saw a movement at an upstairs window.

"Mum, wait!" I cried and opened the car door. "Look. Look at the window."

Ellie had seen it too and had opened her door.

"Both of you, stop it!" Mum said. "What if I'd driven off just then with you both trying to get out of the car?"

I was about to shut the car door when all of sudden, there she was! Misty. Her paws up on the glass. "Mum! Look! It's Misty. I can *see* her."

Mum leaned over and looked back up at the house. "Where? I can't see anything."

"Upstairs window, Mrs Muller," Ellie said. "The one with the blue curtains."

Mum got out of the car and we followed, as if we really were hot-shot detectives. "Goodness, you're right," she said. "It *is* Misty."

Misty had both paws up at the window now and was scrabbling as if she was trying to get out. We ran into the front garden and this time Mum didn't try and stop us because she was jumping up and down with us.

"Misty, Misty," I called up to the window.

We were so excited that we didn't notice the people who had come up behind us.

"What do you think you're doing on my property?" a voice said.

I turned to see a man and a teenage boy, who looked so alike they must be father and son. The teenager was the boy from my dream.

"Ryan!" I cried.

He looked surprised. "How do you know my name? I don't know you."

I pointed at the window. "My cat, she's my cat," I said.

Ryan glanced up at the window then back at me. "Prove it," he said.

I didn't like his tone even though he was just as cute as he'd been in the dreams.

"It's obvious, isn't it? She recognises me."

"That proves nothing," Ryan said. "She's friendly to everyone."

"OK, so how long have you had her?"

"A few weeks. And I don't like your tone."

"I don't like yours either," I said. "A few weeks is exactly how long my cat's been missing." I felt my fists clench. "And now you'd better give her back to me."

"Now then," the man said. "Why doesn't everyone calm down and talk about this like sensible people?"

"Yes," Mum said. "I do apologise for how this might look, but the cat belongs to my daughter and she's been very distressed at her loss."

"There's still no need to be rude," Ryan said.

I stuck my tongue out at him. He stuck his out at me.

Ellie laughed. "I can see you two have hit it off," she said.

"As *if*," we chanted.

"We don't mean to appear difficult," the man said, "but a few people have called since we put up notices about the cat and that made us suspicious. She is such a pretty kitten and we didn't want to hand her over to just anyone."

"Quite right," Ellie said.

"So why don't you come inside and we'll talk this over," the man said. He opened the door and Mum followed him inside. I was about to go with them when Ryan pulled me back.

"You're going to have to prove she's yours," he said. "I mean it."

I made myself take a deep breath. "Her name is Misty."

"That means nothing," Ryan said. "She doesn't have a collar so you could be making up the name. Have you any photos of her?"

I felt myself getting impatient again. "At home, not on me. And she *is* called Misty. I know who you are too. Your name is Ryan and your initials are R.C."

"How do you know that?"

"She has dreams about you," Ellie said.

Ryan raised an eyebrow and looked at me as if I was the maddest person on the planet. "A lot of girls do."

"You're full of yourself as well as rude," I said.

Ellie butted in before I could say anything else to annoy Ryan. "We saw your painting in the shop in town," she said. "The painting of

Misty. You know, the one in the Valentine's competition."

"Anyone could have seen that and made up a story to get the kitten," Ryan said. "But ... hang on, how did you know *I* did that painting?"

"You did a painting that's on the wall in a hotel in Larkspur too," I said.

"Oh yeah, I did that for one of Dad's customers ages ago – but how do you know about it? And don't tell me you dreamed it. Have you been stalking me?"

"In your dreams," I said.

"No, in *your* dreams, you say," he replied and I couldn't help but laugh because it did sound funny. Ryan looked at Ellie. "Are you both crazy or just her?" he asked.

"Both of us," Ellie replied, cool as anything. "We've been following clues. And she did

dream it. After Misty disappeared. She
starting having dreams –"

"And you were in them," I butted in, "and
your painting at the hotel. When we saw it in
real life, we realised you were real and we went
looking for you in art galleries and then I did a
poem about Misty and –"

Ryan's face changed. "Really?" he said, in a
much softer voice. "The poem in the gift shop
window?"

I could see we had his attention now. "Yes.
I got Misty for Valentine's Day last year and
Ellie said I should do a poem about her."

"I saw that poem," he said. "It made me
think. Most of the entries are about people, but
your poem made me realise I could enter my
painting of the kitten."

"*My* kitten," I said.

Ellie looked like she was going to burst with excitement. "Don't you get it?" she said. "We saw your painting and that led us to you."

"Sounds bonkers to me," Ryan said.

"So?" said Ellie. "Doesn't mean it's not true."

Ryan was looking more confused by the second.

"Hold on a minute," I said. "Mum will have a photo of Misty on her phone. She took one for the 'Missing' posters we made to put on lamp-posts."

The front door was open so I went in and found Mum talking to Ryan's dad. "Mum, do you still have that photo of Misty on your phone?" I asked.

"I ... I think so. Hold on." She got out her mobile and scrolled up until she found it.

Ryan went over and nodded. His shoulders dropped and he looked sad. "Looks like she is yours," he said. "It's just ... well ... we've grown very fond of her."

"Where did you find her?" Mum asked him kindly.

"She just appeared one day," Ryan's dad said. "I do gardening work all over town. The back of my van's always open so I can get to my tools. We reckon she popped in there one day, tucked herself up in a corner and fell asleep. I retraced my steps and we put up a few posters but, that's just it. We had such a response – six people, would you believe? In the end, we didn't know who to believe so we took the posters down after a few days."

"I'm glad you did," I said. "But didn't you see ours where we live?"

"I'm afraid not," the man said. "I drive all over in my van and I can't stop to look at every poster ..."

Misty must have heard our voices in the hall because just then she appeared at the top of the stairs and let out a loud meow.

"Misty," I cried.

She meowed again then came scampering down the stairs, took a graceful leap and landed right in my arms. Everyone was looking at me, but still my eyes filled with tears. Misty was OK and I had her back. It felt like the best day of my whole life.

CHAPTER 7
Result

On the way home, we stopped at a pet shop and Mum bought four new collars with name tags attached.

"We're not taking any chances," she said, and she handed them to me as she got back to the car.

As soon as we got Misty home, I wrote her name on one of the tags and put a collar round her neck. She seemed so pleased to be back. She ran around and sniffed all her familiar places, then she settled onto my lap where she purred and nuzzled my hand.

After a few minutes, my phone beeped. It was a message from Ryan. It said –

Your mate gave me your number. Hope you don't mind. Is Misty OK?

I took a snap of her and sent it to him.

He messaged back – ☺ **she's OK.** ☹ **miss her**.

I messaged – **You can visit her**.

He messaged back – ☺☺☺

'Maybe he's not so bad after all,' I thought as I settled down with Misty again.

*

The next day when I got back from school, Mum was waiting in the kitchen with a smug look on her face.

"There's been a special delivery," she said and handed me an envelope.

Inside was a card with a kitten on the front. Not Misty, but a cat with silvery fur just like hers.

It said –

Roses are red,
Violets are blue,
Your cat's a real cutie
And so, Marcie, are you.

It was signed with one X and in brackets – (sorry it's a day late!)

"A mystery admirer?" Mum said with a grin.

"Oh no," I said. "No mystery. I know exactly who it's from."

My first Valentine.

I ran with it up to my room and then went to tell Ellie.

Our books are tested
for children and young people by
children and young people.

Thanks to everyone who consulted on
a manuscript for their time and effort in
helping us to make our books better
for our readers.